Claire Freedman
& Carrie May

DREAMWEAVER

When night shadows fall, and the moonlight gleams,
The dreamweaver comes with her sack full of dreams.
Dreams that she's chosen and woven with care,
For each little creature who's sleepy somewhere.

To Betty with love
C.F.
For Jon and for my parents, Bob and Chris
C.M.

t

templar publishing

A TEMPLAR BOOK

First published in the UK in 2017 by Templar Publishing,
an imprint of Kings Road Publishing, part of the Bonnier Publishing Group,
The Plaza, 535 King's Road, London, SW10 0SZ
www.bonnierpublishing.com

ISBN 978-1-78370-798-0 (Hardback)
ISBN 978-1-78370-799-7 (Paperback)

Designed by Genevieve Webster
Edited by Alison Ritchie

Printed in China

On magical mountain-tops sprinkled with snow,
She gathers the flowers that secretly grow,
Then scoops up soft snowflakes that settle so deep
And weaves them together for one dreamy sleep.

"Who needs my dream?" the dreamweaver sighs,
A sparkle of starlight shines in her eyes.
The dreamweaver sees Little Bear is awake,
She looks in her sack, she gives it a shake.

"Here's a dream, Little Bear, a dream just for you,
Filled with magic, surprises and wishes come true!"

"Dream, Little Bear, that you tread your feet
On crags where the clouds and the mountains meet.
Slide down the slopes in the silver light,
And play with the snowbears, all through the night."

On goes the dreamweaver, travelling far.
From high in the heavens, she pulls down a star,
Glittering comet trails, dust from the moon,
She'll weave someone sleepy a dream very soon.

Little Tiger is yawning and ready for bed.
The Dreamweaver smiles, "Here's your dream, sleepyhead.
With starlight and sparkles, I wove it for you,
So now you'll sleep soundly all the night through."

"Dream, Little Tiger, of flying to Space,
Up to the stars, in a comet race.
Wave to the Earth as you float on by,
Around and around the moon you fly!"

On goes the dreamweaver, hoping to find
Magical dream-stuff of every kind.
She travels to places that no one else knows,
Filling her sack wherever she goes.

Grains of sand on a distant shore,
Pink pearly shells from the ocean floor.
Long-lost treasure, a mermaid's kiss,
The shimmering scales from a rainbow fish.

"Who needs my dream?" the dreamweaver sighs,
A twinkle of moonlight shines in her eyes.
Little Monkey is sleepy and starting to snore.
The dreamweaver looks in her sack once more.

"I've a dream, Little Monkey, a dream made for you.
In magical dreams all your wishes come true!"

"Dream, Little Monkey, you're under the sea,
Swimming with dolphins, wild and free.
Play in the water, all the night long,
And dance with delight to the mermaid's song."

The dreamweaver smiles in the dusky light.
There's one last dream to weave tonight.

Shiny, bright raindrops caught from above,
Snowy-white feathers, dropped by a dove.
Soft fluffs of cloud, a wish that's come true,
And a gently whispered 'I love you'.

The Dreamweaver gives her sack one last shake,
Glittering dream-dust trails in her wake.
"Sweet dreams!" she whispers, "to YOU, little one."
Then she slips away,

for her work is done.